U0016783

《吳炳鍾英語教室》系列

吳炳鍾、李怡慧◎著

TABLE OF CONTENTS
目次

英語基礎會話600

英語基礎會話600

GREETING
問候語

整天的問候語

（是問候語，同時也是回答。）

1. Good morning.

早安（上午）。

2. Good afternoon.

午安（中午過後，到黃昏）。

3. Good day.

日安（白天任何時候的問候語與道別語）。

4. Good evening.

晚安（黃昏起）。

5. Hello.

你好（任何時間都可以用的問好）。

*Good night.（見Unit 3）晚安（下午6點以後，與人分手時的
道別語；或晚上睡覺前）。

最常看到的問候語

6. How are you?

你好嗎？

英語基礎會話600

7. I'm fine. Thank you. How are you?

    我很好。 謝謝你。 你好嗎?

8. Fine, thank you.

    好,謝謝你。

9. How are you, Peter?

    彼得,你好嗎?

10. I'm fine. Thank you, and you?

    我很好,謝謝你。你呢?

11. Fine, thanks.

    好,謝謝。

非常正式的問候語

12. How do you do?

    ＊你好。

13. How do you do? It's a pleasure meet-
    ing you.

    你好。很榮幸認識你。

＊非常正式的問候語,而且近來比較少用。適用在很正式的場
  合,與人首次見面,互相認識時用的。 可以在說的同時握手
  及交換名片。
  It's a pleasure meeting you. 中的 a pleasure, 如果覺得太難
  念,可以用 nice 來替代。 變成 It's nice meeting you. (很高
  興認識你。)

英語基礎會話600

與熟識朋友的問候語

14. Hi.*

嗨！你好。

*非常口語的問候語。與Hello 的用法一樣。
通常是與熟識的人，或在比較隨性的場合使用的。與認識的
人再次見面的開場白。

15. I haven't seen you for a long time.

我很久沒有看到你了。

16. I'm glad to see you again.

我很高興能再見到你。

問候朋友的近況及簡答

（以下10組回答是由很好到很不好，以供參考比較）

17. How's your day?

你今天好嗎？

18. Great!

非常好。

19. How's everything?

一切都好嗎？

20. Good.

很好。

21. How's the family?

家裡的人都好嗎？

22. Fine, thank you for asking. How's yours?

很好，謝謝你。你家裡的人呢？

23. How's business?

生意好嗎？

24. Not too bad.

還不錯。

25. How's it going?

一切都進行得好嗎？

26. Ok.

還可以。

27. What's new with you?

有沒有什麼新鮮事？

28. Nothing special.

沒什麼特別的。

29. What are you doing these days?

你（近來）都在做什麼？

30. The same.

老樣子。

31. How are things?

一切都好嗎？

32. Not so good.

不是很好。

33. How have you been?

（近來）好嗎？/ 你一向可好？

34. Not so well, I have a cold.

不太好，我感冒了。

35. How's your dinner?

你的晚餐好吃嗎？

36. Lousy.

非常糟糕。

下面所列是很口語的問法

37. What's up?

怎麼樣啊？

（有時更簡單，講出來只聽到 s'up）

英語基礎會話600

38. What's new?

有什麼新鮮事？

英語基礎會話600

INTRODUCTION
介紹

簡單的自我介紹

39. Hello, I'm Linda.

你好，我是 / 我叫琳達。

40. Hello, my name is Michael Lin.

你好，我的名字是林麥克。

* name可能只指姓、名、或指全名。全名又稱 full name。
last name、family name、或surname 都是姓氏的意思。
first name、given name 是指名字（不包含姓氏）。

第一次見面的自我介紹

41. Hello. I'm Linda Wang. Pleased to meet you.

你好，我是 / 我叫王琳達。 很高興認識你。

42. It's nice meeting you, too.

我也很高興認識你。

* 發音小點子：pleased 的d 和 to 的 t 省略成一個音。 meet
you 變成 mee ju。 My name is... 變成 My na mis...。

介紹他人

43. This is Christine.

這位是克莉絲汀。

44. Hi, Christine, I'm Michael. Nice to meet you.

嗨！克莉絲汀，我是麥克。很高興認識你。

45. Nice to meet you too, Michael.

（我也）很高興認識你，麥克。

介紹第三者給長輩、長官、或在比較正式的場合與答覆

46. I'd like you to meet Professor Wu.

我來介紹吳教授讓您認識。

47. It's an honor to meet you, professor.

非常榮幸認識你，教授。

48. Miss Lin, let me introduce Mrs. Johnson.

林小姐，讓我來介紹強森夫人。

49. It's a pleasure to meet you, Mrs. Johnson.

很常榮幸認識你，強森夫人。

英語基礎會話600

SAYING GOODBYE
道別

一般說法

50. Goodbye.

再會！

51. Good night.

晚安。（夜晚與人分手時，或要睡覺前的道別）。

52. Bye-bye!

再見！（通常是小孩，親密的朋友，及女性所常

用的）。

準備離去（正式及很禮貌的用法）

53. It was nice talking to you.

很愉快與你交談。

54. It was nice meeting you.

很愉快認識你。

55. It was nice to see you again.

很高興再見到你。

準備分手

56. Are we ready to go?

我們可以走了嗎？

57. I have to leave now.

我現在得走了。

58. I must be going now.

我不能不走了。

與熟識的友人道別──並很快會再見面

59. See you later.

待會兒見。

60. See you soon.

很快再見。

61. See you tomorrow.

明天見。

62. See you next week.

下禮拜見。

63. See you then.

到時候見。

64. See you around.

再見（可能隨時都會遇見）。

65. See you.

一會兒見（see ya'是口語化的寫法）。

66. Take care.

保重（全句應是Take care of yourself. 照顧你自己。也等於中文的「保重」）。

臨別用語

67. Keep in touch.

保持聯絡。

68. Talk to you later.

再聯絡。

臨別前的祝福語

69. Have a nice day!

祝你有個美好的一天。

70. Have a good time.

玩得愉快。

英語基礎會話600

71. Have fun.

好好地玩。

72. Have a nice evening.

祝你有個美好的夜晚。

73. Have a great trip.

祝你有個非常好的旅途。

74. Bon Voyage!

祝你旅行快樂。（法語）

Unit 4. SAYING THANK YOU
道謝

一般道謝 / 得到他人的協助，或讚美等

75. Thank you.

謝謝你。

76. You're welcome.

不用客氣。

77. Thanks.

謝了。

78. Sure.

應該的。

79. Thank you very much.

很（非常）謝謝你。

向幫助你的人道謝及回答

80. Thank you very much for your help.

很感謝你給我的幫助。

81. No problem.

沒問題。

82. Thank you for helping us.

謝謝你的幫助。

83. It's my pleasure.

（不要客氣）榮幸之至。

84. Thank you. That's very nice of you.

謝謝你。你真好。

85. It's nothing.

沒什麼。

86. Thank you. I really appreciate it.

謝謝你。我非常地感激。

87. It's nothing at all.

實在算不得什麼。

88. I don't know how to thank you enough.

我不知道該如何謝你。

89. Don't mention it.

不用客氣。（不值一提。）

90. Thanks for everything.

一切都謝謝你。

91. You are quite welcome.

請不要客氣。

92. That's very kind of you.

你（那樣做）真是好心（或慷慨）。

93. Not at all.

不謝。

APOLOGIZING
道歉

一般道歉——犯錯或失禮時，適合任何時候及場合

94. Sorry.

對不起。

95. That's okay.

沒關係。

96. Excuse me.

對不起；不好意思。

97. No problem.

沒問題。

98. Excuse me for a moment.

對不起，我失陪一下。

99. Sure.

請便。

100. Excuse me for being late.

我遲到了。請原諒。

101. That's ok.

沒關係。

102. Will you excuse me, please?

對不起，我必須走了（或必須走開）。對不起，失陪。

103. Of course.

當然。

104. May I be excused?

我可以離席嗎？

105. Yes, you may.

可以。

106. Pardon me.

對不起。

107. I beg your pardon.

對不起。

108. Excuse me, are you Mrs. May?

對不起，你是 Mrs. May 嗎？

109. Yes, I am.

我是。

英語基礎會話600

110. Excuse me, do you have the time?

對不起，你知道現在的時間嗎？

111. Sorry, I don't.

對不起，我不知道。

112. Excuse me, is this yours?

對不起，這是你的嗎？

113. No, it isn't.

不是。

114. Excuse me, is this seat taken?

對不起，這座位有人坐嗎？

115. No, it's not.

沒有。

正式的道歉與答覆

116. I'm (very) sorry.

（非常地）對不起。

117. That's okay.

沒關係。

118. I apologize.

我很抱歉。

119. I'm sorry; I'm late.

對不起，我遲到了

120. Don't worry about it.

沒關係。不要為這件事擔心。

121. Please accept my apologies.

請接受我（所有的）道歉。

122. Apologies accepted.

我接受。

123. Please forgive me.

請原諒我。

124. I forgive you.

我原諒你。

125. Please apologize for me.

請代我說抱歉。

126. I will.

我會的。

127. I'm sorry I couldn't return your call.

很抱歉我不能回你的電話。

128. It doesn't matter.

不要緊。沒有關係。

129. I'm sorry I didn't call you yesterday.

很抱歉我昨天沒打電話給你。

130. Never mind.

沒有關係。

LANGUAGE DIFFICULTIES

溝通困難

表達語言及溝通上的困難

· 沒有聽清楚或沒聽懂別人對你說的話時。

131. Excuse me?

對不起（你説什麼？）。（把尾音提高）

132. Pardon?

對不起（你説什麼？）。（把尾音提高）

133. I beg your pardon?

非常抱歉（你説什麼？）。（把尾音提高）

· 非常口語的，也比較簡單的説法。說的時候也把音調提高，表示問句。

134. Huh?

（什麼？）

135. What?

什麼？

136. Say again?

再說一次。

英語基礎會話600

137. Again, please.

請再說一次。

138. What did you say?

你剛剛說什麼？

請對方再說一次（有禮貌的問法）

139. Please repeat what you said.

請把你的話重複一遍。

140. Please say that again.

請再說一次。

表達自己的語言困難

141. I can't speak English.

我不會講英文。

142. I'm sorry. I don't understand.

對不起，我聽不懂。

143. I'm sorry. I don't understand English.

對不起，我不懂英文。

144. I'm sorry. I don't speak any English.

對不起，我（完全）不會講英文。

145. My English isn't very good.

我的英文不是很好。

請對方修正語速 / 音量

146. Please say it more slowly.

請說得再慢一點。

147. Please speak a little more slowly.

請說得再慢一點。

148. Please speak slower.

請說得慢一點。

149. Please speak louder.

請說得大聲一點。

150. Could you speak a little louder?

可不可以請你大聲一點？

151. Speak up, please.

請大聲說。（口語用法）

152. I'm sorry; I can't hear you.

對不起，我聽不見你（說的話）。

做進一步的溝通

153. Do you speak Chinese?
你會講中文嗎？

154. Do you speak any Japanese?
你會說日文嗎？

155. How do you say this in English?
這個怎麼用英文說？

156. How do you pronounce this word?
這個字要怎麼念？

157. How do you spell that word?
那個字怎麼拼？

158. What does it mean?
那是什麼意思？

159. What's the meaning of this word?
這個字是什麼意思？

160. I don't know.
我不知道。

161. Do you understand it?
你懂了嗎？

162. I don't understand.

我不懂。

163. I understand it now.

我現在懂了。

164. I understand you, but I don't know how to answer.

我懂得你的意思，但我不會回答。

較口語的回答

165. I see what you mean.

我瞭解你的意思。

166. I see.

我瞭解了。

167. I got it.

我懂了。

Unit 7. ASKING & OFFERING HELP
請求幫助／伸出援手

請求幫助

168. Can you help me?
你能幫我嗎？

169. Sure. What can I do?
當然。 我能做什麼？

170. Can someone help me?
有人可以幫我嗎？

171. Of course. Let me help you.
當然。讓我幫你。

172. Would you give me a hand, please?
請你幫我一下。

173. Would you help me, please?
請幫我好嗎？

伸出援手

174. Let me help you.

讓我幫你。

175. Thank you very much.

非常謝謝你。

176. Let me give you a hand.

讓我來（幫你）。

177. That's very nice of you.

你真好。

178. I'm fine.

我可以（我不需要幫助）。

179. Can I help you?

能幫你嗎？

180. Yes, thank you.

可以，謝謝。

181. No, thank you.

不用，謝謝。

英語基礎會話600

在商店購物時的對話

182. May I help you?

我能爲你服務嗎？

183. Yes, I'd like to look at that red sweater.

我想看看那一件紅色的毛衣。

184. May I help you with something?

有什麼能爲你服務嗎？

185. No, I'm just looking.

不用。我只是看看。

LOOKING FOR THE RESTROOM
找廁所

找廁所

186. Excuse me. Could you tell me where the restroom is?

對不起。請你告訴我洗手間在哪裡，好嗎？

可以代換的辭彙

washroom 盥洗室

men's room 男廁所

ladies' room 女廁所

powder room 化妝室（女士的說法）

bathroom 洗澡間（在家裡的）

toilet 廁所（toilet 在美國是指馬桶）

lavatory 盥洗室（在飛機上的稱呼）

W.C.：water closet 的縮寫（是美國沒有的說法）

HEALTH
健康

187. Where can I find a doctor?

我可以在哪裡找到（一位）醫生？

188. Where is the drug store?

藥房在哪裡？

189. Do you need a doctor?

你需要看醫生嗎？

190. Yes, I need a doctor.

是的，我需要一位醫生。

191. Are you all right?

你還好嗎？

192. I'm not feeling very well.

我不太舒服。

193. I don't feel very well.

我感覺不適。

194. Do you need to go to the hospital?

你需要去醫院嗎？

195. I think I'm sick.

我可能生病了。

196. Where can I buy some cold medicine?

我可以在哪兒買到感冒藥？

197. Are you injured?

你有受傷嗎？

198. Yes, I'm hurt.

是的，我受傷了。

199. Are you hurt?

你受傷了嗎？

200. No, I'm okay.

沒有，我沒事。

201. Does this hurt?

這樣會痛嗎？

202. Yes, it hurts.

會痛。

203. Yes, it does.

會。

204. Can you call an ambulance?

你可以叫部救護車嗎？

205. Can someone call 911?

有誰可以幫忙打119嗎？（美國的緊急電話是911）

英語基礎會話600

Unit 10. MONEY
金錢

問價錢（和數字的説法）。（注意數字的發音／重音）

206. How much is it?

這個多少錢？（單數）

207. Seventy cents.

0.7元。

208. How much are they?

這些多少錢？（複數）

209. Seventeen dollars, altogether.

一共17元。

210. What's the price?

價錢是多少？

211. How much did it cost?

價錢是多少？

212. Thirty dollars.

30元。

English conversation

book

Unit 10. MONEY 金錢

Unit 10. MONEY
金錢

問價錢（和數字的説法）。（注意數字的發音／重音）

206. How much is it?

這個多少錢？（單數）

207. Seventy cents.

0.7元。

208. How much are they?

這些多少錢？（複數）

209. Seventeen dollars, altogether.

一共17元。

210. What's the price?

價錢是多少？

211. How much did it cost?

價錢是多少？

212. Thirty dollars.

30元。

英語基礎會話600

213. What's the charge?

費用是多少？

214. Thirteen dollars.

13元。

215. How much for a dozen?

一打（十二個）多少錢？

216. Fourteen dollars and forty cents.

14.4元。

217. How much are these?

這些要多少錢？

218. Fifteen dollars and fifty cents.

15.5元。

219. How much do I owe you?

我要付你多少錢？（我欠你多少錢？）

220. Sixteen dollars and sixty cents.

16.6元。

221. How much for everything?

全部多少錢？

英語基礎會話600

222. Eighteen dollars and eighty cents.

18.8元。

223. What's the total?

一共是多少？

224. The total comes to nineteen dollars and ninety cents.

一共是19.9元。

225. What's the fare?

車錢是多少？

226. The total comes to twelve twenty-two.

總計一共是12.22元。

227. Cash or charge?

（付帳時店員問：）付現還是刷卡？

228. Cash.

付現。

229. I want to pay by credit card.

我要用信用卡付錢。

230. I want to charge it（to my credit card）.

我要用信用卡付錢。

231. Please charge this to my room.

請把這筆帳算到我的（旅館）房間的帳上。

232. Do you accept（take）traveler's checks?

你收旅行支票嗎？

常用貨幣的說法

233. This is...U.S. Dollars.

這個是……美元。

＊Yuan 人民幣

Yen 日圓

Euro 歐元

NT Dollars 新台幣

找錢

234. Here's your change.

這是找你的錢。

235. Keep the change.

不用找了。（給人小費時說的）

無法找零時

236. I have no change.

我沒有零錢。

237. Sorry, I don't have any change.

對不起，我沒有零錢。

需要換錢時

238. Do you have change for a hundred dollar bill?

你能不能找開100元的鈔票？

239. Do you have change for a fifty?

能不能向你換50元的零錢？

240. Can you break a hundred（dollar bill）?

你能不能找開100元的鈔票？

＊以上三句的簡答都可以用 sure（當然），yes（可以），或 Sorry, I can't.（對不起，沒辦法。）來回答。

討價還價

241. This is too expensive.

這個太貴了。

242. Can you give me a discount?

可不可以打個折給我？

243. Do you have something less expensive?

有沒有沒那麼貴的？

244. It this on sale?

這個有打折嗎？

英語基礎會話600

DATE
日期

日期的說法

245. What's today's date?

今天的日期是什麼？

246. Today is the first.

今天是1號。

247. Is today the fifteenth?

今天是15號嗎？

248. Today is February, 15th.

今天是2月15日。

249. What date is today?

今天是幾號？

250. It's the 10th of October.

10月10號。

251. It's October 10th.

10月10號。

252. What date of the month is it?

今天是（這個月的）幾號？

253. It's the first.

1號。

星期幾的說法

254. What day is it?

今天是星期幾？

255. It's Wednesday.

今天是星期三。

256. What day is today?

今天是星期幾？

257. Today is Friday.

今天是星期五。

258. What day is this?

今天是星期幾？

259. Thursday.

星期四。

260. What day of the week is this?

今天是（本週的）星期幾？

261. Tuesday.

　　星期二。

問特定日子

262. What day is Christmas this year?

　　今年的聖誕節是星期幾？

263. Christmas is on a Saturday this year.

　　今年的聖誕節是個星期六。

264. When is your birthday?

　　你的生日是哪一天？

265. My birthday is March 23rd.

　　我的生日是3月23號。

266. I was born on August 11th.

　　我的生日是8月11號。

267. I was born in 1967.

　　我是1967年出生的。

詢問時間 & 時間的說法

268. What time is it?

現在幾點？

269. It's 8 o'clock.

8點鐘。

270. Do you have the time?

你知道現在的時間嗎？

271. Yes, it's nine thirty.

現在9點半。

272. What time do you have?

你的表幾點了？

273. It's eleven twenty.

11點20分。

274. It's twenty minutes after eleven.

11點20分。

275. It's half past twelve.

12點半。

276. It's five after eleven.

11點5分。

277. It's a quarter to eleven.

差一刻鐘11點。

278. It's a quarter of eleven.

差一刻鐘11點。

279. Ten in the morning.

上午10點。

280. Six in the afternoon.

下午6點。

281. Eight in the evening.

晚上8點。

282. Do you know the time?

你知道現在幾點嗎？

283. It's five minutes to six.

再5分鐘6點。

英語基礎會話600

284. It's ten minutes to four.

差10分4點。

285. Ten to four.

差10分4點。

286. Do you have the correct time?

你知道正確的時間嗎？

287. It's a quarter after seven.

7點1刻。

288. Would / Could you tell me what time it is?

能不能請你告訴我現在的時間？

289. It's 8:01.

8點零一分。

290. Could you give me the time?

你能告訴我現在的時間嗎？

291. It's almost 9 o'clock.

快9點了。

292. May I have the time?

請問現在的時間？

293. It's just after 10.

剛過10點。

294. Sorry, but I don't have a watch.

對不起，我沒戴表。

295. Sorry, I don't have the time.

對不起，我不知道現在的時間。

296. What time do you have?

你的表是幾點？

297. What time is the meeting?

幾點鐘開會？

298. The meeting is at 3:30.

3點半開會。

299. What time does the meeting start?

會議什麼時候開始？

300. The meeting will start at 2 o'clock sharp.

會議兩點整開始。

301. When is the meeting?

會議是什麼時候開？

302. The meeting is tomorrow afternoon at 3.

會議是明天下午3點鐘開。

WEATHER
氣候

303. What's the weather like?

天氣怎麼樣？

304. It's sunny.

是晴天。

305. How's the weather?

氣候如何？

306. It's warm.

蠻溫暖的。

307. What's the temperature today?

今天氣溫幾度？

308. It's 23 degrees Celsius.

攝氏23度。

309. It's 74 degrees Fahrenheit.

華氏74度。

有關氣候的閒聊

310. It's a lovely day.

今天（天氣）很好。

311. The weather is nice today.

今天的天氣不錯。

312. It's a hot day.

今天相當熱。

313. How chilly it is!

真冷！

314. There's a typhoon coming.

有颱風要來了。

315. Warm day, isn't it?

天氣好暖和啊！

316. How do you like the weather?

你覺得天氣怎麼樣？

317. Just fine.

頗好。

318. Not bad.

不壞。

319. It's awful.

太壞了。

320. It's terrible.

糟透了。

321. Do you think it's going to rain?

你認為要下雨了嗎？

322. I don't think it's going to rain.

我認為不會下雨。

Unit 14. TELEPHONE

電話

接起電話時

323. Hello?

喂？

打電話找人

324. Hello. Is Nancy there, please?

喂，請問南西在嗎？

325. Yes, she is. Just a moment, please.

她在，請等一下。

326. Hello. Is this Peter?

喂，你是彼得嗎？

327. Yes, this is he.

我是。

328. Hello. May I speak with Peter?

喂，我想和彼得說話。

329. Speaking.

我就是。

330. Is Dr. Howard in?

Howard 醫生在嗎？

331. Yes, hold on.

在，等一下。

332. May I speak to Lucy, please?

我想和Lucy說話。

333. Who is this speaking?

請問你是哪位？

334. This is Peter Wang. I'm returning her call.

我是王彼得。我回她的電話。

說明自己的身分

335. This is Mary. May I speak to Jane, please?

我是 Mary，我想找 Jane。

336. One moment, please.

請等一下。

打電話要找的人不在

337. May I speak with Peter, please?

請問彼得在嗎?

338. I'm sorry; but Peter is not in.

對不起,彼得不在。

339. Is Mr. Cline in?

請問Cline先生在嗎?

340. I'm sorry; Mr. Cline is not in his office at the moment.

對不起,Cline先生現在不在他的辦公室。

341. May I speak with Angela?

我想和Angela說話。

342. Angela is not home right now.

Angela 現在不在家。

在工作場所接電話

343. Asia Trading Co., James speaking.

亞洲貿易公司,我是 James。

344. Dr. Yen's office, Miss White speaking.

Dr. Yen的辦公室(診所),(我是)Miss White。

345. Accounting department, Lily speaking.

會計部，（我是）Lily。

346. Good morning. Ace Construction Company. May I help you?

早安。Ace工程公司。請問您有什麼事？

請接線員為你轉接

347. Extension 603, please.

請接分機603號。

348. Mr. Cline's office, please.

請接Cline先生的辦公室。

在旅館裡用內線電話

349. The beauty shop, please.

請接美容院。

350. Room 1425, please.

請接1425號房。

351. May I have the front desk?

請幫我接到櫃檯。

352. May I have the barber shop?

請接理容院。

353. (Operator:) Please hold.

（總機：）請等一下。　（請在線上等一下。）

留言

354. My father is not here. May I take a message?

我的父親不在這裡。請您留話好嗎？

355. Would you like to leave a message?

您要不要留話？

356. Please tell him Peter Wang has called and will call again this evening.

請告訴他，Peter Wang打了電話來，我晚上還會再打來。

357. Will you please take a message?

我可不可以請你留話？

358. Please ask Miss Walker to call Helen Sweet. My phone number is 8936-1212.

請告訴 Miss Walker 打電話給 Helen Sweet （即留話的本人）。我的電話是8936-1212。

電話答錄機

359. You have reached 5787-2824. We can't answer the phone right now. Please leave a message after the 'beep', and we'll get back to you as soon as possible. Thank you.

這裡是5787-2824。我們現在不能接電話。請在嗶聲後留言，我們會盡快與您聯絡。謝謝。

打錯電話

360. I think you have the wrong number.

我想你撥錯了號碼。

361. What number are you calling?

你打多少號？（你撥幾號？）

362. Is this 2321-3295?

這裡是2321-3295嗎？

363. No, it isn't.

不是。

364. Sorry, I've got the wrong number.

抱歉，我打錯了。

365. There's no one here by that name.

這裡沒有這個人。

366. I'm sorry. I must have the wrong number.

抱歉，我一定是弄錯了號碼。

367. You have the wrong number.

你打錯了。

368. Sorry to bother you.

抱歉，打擾了。

打國際長途電話

369. I'd like to make an overseas call to Los Angeles, please.

我要打一個國際電話到洛杉磯。

370. Operator, I'd like to place an overseas collect call, please.

總機，我要打一個對方付費的國際電話。

371. The number in Taipei is 2551-9143. The country code is 886. The city code is 2.

台北的電話號碼是2551-9143，國碼是886，區碼是2。

372. The party I want is Mr. Lee. My name is Wang, spelled W-A-N-G.

我要找李先生。我姓王，拼法是W-A-N-G。

EATING
用餐

用餐訂位

373. I'd like to make a reservation.

我要訂位。

374. Your name and how many in your party, please?

（請問）你的名字和幾個人？

375. My name is Jake Lee. It's dinner for 5 at 7 p.m. tomorrow night.

我的名字是Jake Lee。（一共）5個人，明天晚上
7點的晚餐。

在餐廳裡

376. May I see the menu, please?

請給我看菜單。

377. What's today's special?

今天的特餐是什麼？

378. I like to order your sea food special.

我要點你們的海鮮特餐。

379. May I have the check, please?

請給我帳單。

380. Check, please.

買單。

在速食店

381. May I help you?

我能為你服務嗎？（要點什麼？）

382. I would like to order two hamburgers.

我要兩個漢堡。

383. Is that for here, or to go?

內用還是外帶？

384. To go, please.

外帶。

Unit 16. ASKING FOR PERMISSION
徵求同意

385. May / Can I come in?

我可以進來嗎？

386. Yes, you may. （Yes, you can.）

可以。

387. May / Can I use your telephone?

我可以用你的電話嗎？

388. No, you may not. （No, you can't.）

不可以。

389. May / Can I borrow this pencil?

我可以借用這枝鉛筆嗎？

390. Sure.

當然可以。

391. Do you mind if I open the window?

我想開窗，你介意嗎？

392. No, I don't mind.

我不介意。（可以開窗）

393. Would you mind closing the window?

請你關窗，你介意嗎？

394. No, I don't mind.

我不介意。（可以關窗）

395. Will you read that again, please?

請你再讀一遍，好嗎？

396. Sure.

沒問題。

397. May I have a glass of water, please?

請給我一杯水，好嗎？

398. Sure.

當然。

正式的邀請

399. I would like to invite you to a concert this weekend.

我想這個週末請你去（聽）音樂會。

400. I'd like that（very much）.

我非常樂意。

401. Would you like to go out for a drink after work?

下班後願不願意（一起）去喝一杯？

402. No, thanks.（but thanks for asking.）

不，謝謝。（但謝謝你的邀請。）

403. Would you like to join us for lunch?

你要不要和我們一起吃中飯？

404. Yes, I'd love to. Thanks.

非常樂意，謝謝。

405. Would you like to go see a movie this weekend?

這個週末願不願意（和我）看場電影？

402. Sorry, I can't.

對不起，我不能去。

407. We would like to invite you to have dinner with us on Friday.

我們想請你這個禮拜五和我們一起吃晚飯。

408. I'll look forward to it. Thank you.

我會期待的。謝謝。

隨興邀請熟識的朋友

409. Let's go grab some lunch.

一起去吃中飯？

410. Okay.

好啊。

411. Let's go to the ball game this Sunday.

星期天一起去看球賽？

412. That sounds great!

（聽起來）好極了！

413. Let me buy you a drink after work.

下班後讓我請你喝一杯。

414. I'd like to, but I have to work late. Thanks anyway.

我也想，但是我要加班。（無論如何）謝謝了！

祝福

415. Good luck.

祝（你）好運。

416. Best of luck.

祝你有最好的運氣。

417. I wish you luck.

（我）祝你幸運。

418. I hope that everything goes well for you.

（我）希望你一切都順利。

祝賀

419. Happy New Year.

新年快樂。

420. Merry Christmas.

聖誕快樂。

421. Happy birthday to you.

祝你生日快樂。

422. Happy anniversary.

（結婚）紀念日快樂。

423. Congratulations!

恭賀你！恭喜！

424. I wish you happiness!

祝你幸福、快樂。

425. Congratulations on your promotion!

恭喜你升了級。

426. Congratulations on your success!

恭賀你的成功。

稱讚

427. How nice!

太好了！

428. It's so beautiful.

好美！

429. It's marvelous!

太好了！

430. I'm very impressed.

我很佩服（讚賞）。

431. I've really enjoyed the dinner.

我很高興能享受這頓晚餐。

432. I've really enjoyed your talk.

我實在高興能聽到你的演講。

問候

433. Give my regards to your brother.

代我問候你的哥哥（或弟弟）。

434. Please give my best regards to Mrs. Hill.

代我問候Mrs. Hill。

435. Please say hello to Thomas for me.

請代我問候Thomas。

EXPRESSING REGRET
AND SYMPATHY
表示慰問及遺憾

436. How unfortunate!

真是不幸。

437. I'm very sorry to hear that.

這件事讓我聽了很難過。

438. My deepest sympathy.

我感同身受。（我覺得很難過）。

439. If there's anything I can do, please let
me know.

如果我能幫得上什麼忙，請告訴我。

440. That's too bad.

真是不幸。

441. Too bad.

真不幸。

SIMPLE QUESTIONS& ANSWERS
簡單的問題與回答

凡是WH-開頭的問句，一定要回答，不能只用搖頭（不是）或點頭（是）來作答。

WHAT

442. What is his name?

他叫什麼？他姓什麼？他的姓名是什麼？

443. His name is Jeffrey Stone.

他的名字是Jeffrey Stone。

444. What does she want?

她有什麼事？

445. She wants to ask you about something.

她有事情要問你。

446. What happened?

發生了什麼事？

447. There was a car accident.

（那兒）發生了一場車禍。

448. What's the matter with you?

你怎麼了？

449. I'm not feeling very well.

我不大舒服。

450. What are you looking for?

你在找什麼？

451. I'm looking for my car keys.

我在找我的汽車鑰匙。

WHO

452. Who is first?

誰是第一位？（誰先到的？）

453. This lady came first.

這位女士先到的。

454. Who (Whom) do you want to see?

你要找誰？

455. I'm here to see Dr. White.

我來找White醫師。

456. Who (Whom) did you meet today?

你今天遇到誰了？

457. I met with Prof. Brown.

我遇見了Brown教授。

WHEN

458. When will he return?

他幾點鐘回來？

459. He will come back at 4 p.m.

他將在下午4點回來。

460. When does the store close?

店幾點鐘打烊？

461. The store closes at 6 p.m.

店下午6點鐘打烊。

462. When is the plane leaving?

飛機幾時起飛？

463. The plane is leaving at 11:45 a.m.

飛機上午11點45分離開。

464. When did you buy this?

你幾時買這個的？

465. I bought this a long time ago.

我很久以前買的。

466. When was he born?

他何時出生的？

467. He was born in 1962.

他出生於1962年。

468. What date?

哪一天？

469. He was born on August 25th.

他在8月25日出生。

470. When were you born?

你是何時出生的？

471. I was also born in August 1962, but not on the 25th.

我也是1962年8月出生，但不是在25日。

472. When did he leave?

他幾時離開的？

473. He left on December 24th.

他在12月24日離開的。

474. What day was it?

那一天是星期幾？

475. It was Thursday.

是星期四。

WHICH

476. Which bus are we taking?

我們搭哪一輛（一班）巴士？

477. Which one are we taking?

我們搭哪一班？

478. We are taking the No. 11 bus.

我們搭第11路的巴士。

479. Which shirt is better?

哪一件襯衫比較好？

480. Which one is better?

哪一件比較好？

481. The blue shirt is better than the white one.

藍色的那件襯衫比白色的好。

482. Which is your raincoat?

哪一件雨衣是你的？

483. Which one is yours?

哪一件是你的？

484. My raincoat is the red one on the coat rack.

我的雨衣是在衣架上紅色的（那一件）。

485. Which is cheaper, yours or hers?

是你的比較便宜還是她的？

486. Which one is cheaper?

哪一個比較便宜？

487. Mine's cheaper than hers.

我的比她的便宜。

WHERE

488. Where is the Police Station?

警察局在哪裡？

489. The Police Station is on First Street.

警察局在第一街上。

490. Where is John's office?

John 的辦公室在哪裡？

491. It's down the hall, second door on your left.

這個走廊直走，左邊的第二個門。

492. Where is the exit?

出口在哪裡？

493. The exit is at the back of the building.

出口在大樓的後方。

494. Where is the main entrance?

（正門）入口在哪裡？

495. The main entrance is on the first floor.

正門在一樓。

496. Where is the public phone?

公共電話在哪裡？

497. There is a public phone over there.

公共電話在那邊。（指著所說的方向）

498. Where have you been?

你到什麼地方去了？你去過了什麼地方？

499. I was at the coffee shop.

我在咖啡廳裡。

Do / DOES（有沒有）

*可以只用搖頭（不是）或點頭（是）來作答的問答。（Yes / No Questions & Answers）

500. Do you have a card?

你有名片嗎？

501. Yes, here you go.

有，在這兒。

502. Does she have our phone number?

她有我們的電話號碼嗎？

503. No, I don't think she does.

我想她沒有。

504. Did you have time to read the letter?

你有時間看那封信嗎？

505. Yes, I did.

我有（看過了）。

506. Do they have enough money for the tickets?

他們有足夠的錢買票嗎？

507. No, I don't think they do.

我想他們沒有。

Yes / No（是不是）

508. Is Mr. Taylor in the office?
Mr. Taylor 在辦公室嗎？

509. No, he is not.
他不在。

510. Is the manager in?
經理在嗎？

511. Yes, he is.
他在。

512. Was Mrs. Wilson home?
Mrs. Wilson（當時）在家嗎？

513. No, she was not.
她（當時）不在。

514. Are you sure you can go?
你確定你能去嗎？

515. Yes, I'm sure.
我確定。

516. Are you busy?
你忙嗎？

517. No, I'm not.

不，我不忙。

518. Will you be free tomorrow?

你明天有空嗎？

519. Yes, I'm free tomorrow.

我明天有空。

520. Will you go by bus?

你（將會）坐巴士去嗎？

521. Yes, I will.

我會。

522. Are you going by bus?

你坐巴士去嗎？

523. No, I'm not.

我不會。

524. Will he come back this afternoon?

他今天下午回來嗎？

525. Yes, he will.

他會。

526. Is he coming back this afternoon?

他今天下午回來嗎？

527. No, he's not.

他不會。

528. Did you see the show?

你看了表演嗎？

529. Yes, I did.

我看過了。

530. Have you seen the show?

你看了表演嗎？

531. No, I haven't.

我還沒有。

532. Did she finish her work?

她做完工作了嗎？

533. Yes, she did.

她做完了。

534. Has she finished her work?

她做完工作了嗎？

535. No, she hasn't.

她還沒做完。

AGREEING &
DISAGREEING
同意與不同意

同意的表示

536. Yes, certainly.

當然！

537. Yes, I see.

啊！我明白了。

538. Yes, I think so.

對，我想是那樣。

539. I quite agree with you.

我很同意你的意見。

540. I agree.

我同意。

541. You're completely right.

你完全正確。

542. You are correct.

你是正確的。

543. I believe so.

我相信是那樣。

544. So do I.

我也是那樣。（我也那樣想 / 我也要 / 我也喜歡。）

可能贊同

545. I guess so.

我（猜）想是吧。

546. I suppose so.

我想是吧。

懷疑，無把握的表示

547. I'm not sure.

我不能確定。

548. It could be.

是可能的。

549. I doubt it.

我對它（真實性，可能性）懷疑。

550. You don't say!

真的嗎？有這種事？有這種道理？

551. Is that true?

那是真的嗎？

552. It's hard to believe.

難以置信。

553. Really?

真的嗎？

554. Are you sure?

你確定嗎？

不同意的表示

555. Oh, no!

不是的！不要！沒有！

556. No, I don't agree with you.

我不同意你的說法 / 看法。

557. I'm afraid you're mistaken.

恐怕你錯了。

558. I disagree completely.

我完全不同意。

英語基礎會話600

559. I don't think so.

我認為不是那樣。

560. You are wrong.

你錯了。

561. Impossible.

不可能。

562. That's not true.

那不是實情。

563. You must be joking.

你在開玩笑吧？

564. No way!

不可能。

565. Neither do I.

我也不相信／我也不同意／我也不認為如此。

拒絕

566. I don't want any. Thank you.

我不要，謝謝。

567. I'm afraid I can't do it.

恐怕我不能做；恐怕我辦不到。

568. I'm sorry I can't help you.

抱歉我不能幫你忙。

EXPRESSING LIKES, DISLIKES

表達喜好

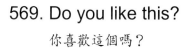

---

569. Do you like this?

你喜歡這個嗎？

570. Yes, I like it very much.

我非常喜歡。

571. No, I really don't like this at all.

我完全不喜歡。

572. Do you like it?

你喜歡（它）嗎？

573. Yes, I like it a lot.

我很喜歡。

574. No, I don't like it.

我不喜歡。

575. Did you enjoy the movie?

你喜歡（觀賞）這部電影嗎？

576. Yes, I really love this movie.

我非常喜愛這部電影。

577. No, I really hate this movie.

我非常厭惡這部電影。

578. How do you like this song?

你覺得這首歌如何？

579. Yes, I love it.

我（很）喜愛它。

580. No, I hate it.

我（很）討厭它。

581. Do you like French Food?

你喜歡法國菜嗎？

582. Yes, I really love it.

我非常喜歡。

583. No, I can't stand it（at all）.

我完全不能忍受。

584. Do you like to watch basketball games?

你喜歡看籃球賽嗎？

585. Yes, I like it.

我喜歡。

586. No, I don't like it very much.

我不是很喜歡。

SMALL TALK
閒話家常

打開話題

587. I'm very interested in learning English.

我對學英文很感興趣。

588. This book is very interesting.

這本書非常有意思。

589. Where are you from?

您從哪兒來的啊？

590. Where do you live?

你住在哪裡？（居住的家在哪？）

591. Where are you staying?

你住在哪裡？（你暫住在哪裡？）

592. Welcome to Taiwan.

歡迎到台灣來。

593. Is this your first trip to Taipei?

這是你第一次來台北嗎？

594. I hope you will enjoy your stay in Taiwan.

我希望您在台灣的停留愉快。

595. Are you enjoying your visit in Taiwan?

你的台灣行愉快嗎？

談天常用的短句

596. It's expensive, isn't it?

真貴啊！

597. It's heavy, isn't it?

很重啊！

598. It's delicious, isn't it?

味道很美啊！

599. You like milk, don't you?

你愛喝牛奶啊！

600. She（sure）likes ice cream, doesn't she?

她真愛吃冰淇淋啊！

英語基礎會話600

601. Wonderful weather we are having, isn't it?

天氣可真美好啊！

JOBS / OCCUPATIONS
職業

602. What is your job?

你的工作是什麼？

603. I'm a doctor.

我是醫生。

604. What is your profession?

你的（專業）職業是什麼？

605. I'm a teacher.

我是老師。

606. What is your occupation?

你的職業是什麼？

607. I'm an electric engineer.

我是電子工程師。

608. What do you do?

你是做什麼的？

609. I'm a student.

我是學生。

610. I own my own printing company.

我擁有自己的印刷公司。

611. I'm helping out in the family business.

我在幫家裡做生意。

612. I'm a house wife.

我是家庭主婦。

613. I'm unemployed.

我失業中。

614. What do you do for a living?

你是以什麼謀生？

615. I work for a software company.

我替一家軟體公司工作。

616. I'm running the family trading business.

我經營家族企業。

617. Where do you work?

你在哪兒工作？

618. I work in Singapore.

我在新加坡工作。

英語基礎會話600

619. I work at the bookstore.

我在書店工作。

620. I work for a local college.

我替當地的大學做事。

621. Who do you work for?

你替誰做事?

622. I work for an American company.

我在一家美國公司做事。

623. I'm with First International Bank.

我在第一國際銀行。

624. What kind of work do you do?

你做哪方面的工作?

625. I'm in banking.

我在銀行界。

626. I'm in computers.

我做電腦（相關的工作）。

627. How long have you worked here?

你在這工作多久了?

628. How long have you had this job?

你做這個工作多久了？

629. How do you like your job?

你覺得你的工作怎樣？

630. Do you enjoy your work?

你喜愛你的工作嗎？

631. How long have you been working as a photographer?

你做攝影師的工作多久了？

HOBBIES & INTERESTS
嗜好及興趣

632. What do you do with your free time?

你有空時都做什麼？

633. How do you spend your weekends?

你如何度過你的週末？

634. What are your hobbies?

你的嗜好是什麼？

635. Do you like sports?

你喜歡體育嗎？

636. Do you like music?

你喜歡音樂嗎？

637. Do you like to dance?

你喜歡跳舞嗎？

638. Do you like to travel?

你喜歡旅行嗎？

639. Do you like to go to the theater?

你喜歡去劇院嗎？

640. Do you like to go to the movies?

你喜歡去看電影嗎？

641. What kind of music do you like?

你喜歡哪種音樂？

642. What kind of sport do you like?

你喜歡哪種運動？

643. What kind of movie do you like?

你喜歡哪種電影？

644. What is your favorite pastime?

你最喜歡的消遣是什麼？

645. What is your favorite food?

你最喜歡的食物是什麼？

646. What is your favorite sport?

你最喜歡的運動 / 體育活動是什麼？

647. What is your favorite kind of music?

你最喜歡的音樂類型是什麼？

648. What is your favorite subject in school?

（在學校裡）你最喜歡的科目是什麼？

英語基礎會話600

SHORT
INSTRUCTIONS
簡短的指示

649. Sit down.

坐下。

650. Stand up.

站起來。

651. Walk this way.

跟我走。往這兒走。

652. Go away.

走開。

653. Leave!

離開。走開。

654. Run!

（快）跑。

655. Stop!

停。

656. Wait!

等一下。

657. Hold it!

別動。

658. Hands up.

把手舉起來。

659. Raise your hand.

請舉手。

660. Line up.

排隊。

661. Get in line.

請排隊。

662. Take a number.

拿一個號碼牌。

663. Next.

下一個人。

664. Shut up!

閉嘴。

665. Don't talk.

別說話。

666. Hush up.

噓！別說話。

667. Pick it up.

撿起來。

668. Throw it out.

丟出去。

669. Take it.

拿去。

670. Leave it.

別動它。

671. Let it go.

把它放開。

672. Drop it.

放下（鬆手）。

673. Come here.

來。

674. Don't do it.

別（那麼）做。

675. Go up.

上去。

676. Go down.

下去。

677. Come on.

來吧。

678. Look!

看！

679. Watch out!

小心。

680. Look out!

小心。

681. Be careful.

小心。

682. Follow me.

跟我來。跟著我。

683. Show me.

「秀」給我看。

684. Wait a minute.

等一下。

685. Let's go.

我們走吧。

附錄

時間用詞（Time of day）

morning 上午	noon 正中午
afternoon 下午	evening 晚間
night 夜晚	mid-night 子夜
tomorrow 明天	today 今天
yesterday 昨天	

this morning	this afternoon
this evening	at noon
at mid-night	tomorrow morning
tomorrow afternoon	tomorrow evening
tomorrow night	yesterday morning
yesterday afternoon	yesterday evening
last nigh	

this week / month / year	這個星期 / 月 / 年
next week / month / year	下個星期 / 月 / 年
last week / month / year	上個星期 / 月 / 年
the day after tomorrow	後天（明天的後一天）
the day before yesterday	前天（昨天的前一天）
the week after next week	下下禮拜

the week before last week　上上禮拜

two weeks from now　兩個禮拜後

two months from now　兩個月後

two years from now　兩年後

two weeks ago　兩個禮拜前

two months ago　兩個月前

two years ago　兩年前

月份（Months of the year）

January 一月 　　　　February 二月

March 三月 　　　　　April 四月

May 五月 　　　　　　June 六月

July 七月 　　　　　　August 八月

September 九月 　　　October 十月

November 十一月 　　December 十二月

星期（Days of the week）

Monday 星期一 　　　Tuesday 星期二

Wednesday 星期三 　Thursday 星期四

Friday 星期五 　　　　Saturday 星期六

Sunday 星期日

英語基礎會話600

數字及序數（Numbers & Ordinal numbers）

1	one	first
2	two	second
3	three	third
4	four	fourth
5	five	fifth
6	six	sixth
7	seven	seventh
8	eight	eighth
9	nine	ninth
10	ten	tenth

11	eleven	eleventh
12	twelve	twelfth
13	thirteen	thirteenth
14	fourteen	fourteenth
15	fifteen	fifteenth
16	sixteen	sixteenth
17	seventeen	seventeenth
18	eighteen	eighteenth
19	nineteen	nineteenth

20	twenty	twentieth
30	thirty	thirtieth
40	forty	fortieth
50	fifty	fiftieth
60	sixty	sixtieth
70	seventy	seventieth
80	eighty	eightieth
90	ninety	ninetieth

21	twenty-one	twenty-first
22	twenty-two	twenty-second
23	twenty-three	twenty-third
24	twenty-four	twenty-fourth

100	one hundred	one hudredth
101	one hundred (and) one	
1,000	one thousand	one thousandth
10,000	ten thousand	
100,000	one hundred thousand	
1,000,000	one million	one millionth

英語基礎會話600

數學上的簡要寫法（Math）

addition　　　加 + plus

One plus one equals（is）2.

subtraction　　減 - minus

Two minus one equals（is）1.

multiplication 乘 X times

Two times two equals（is）4.

division　　　除 / divided by

Two divided by two equals（is）1.

顏色（Colors）

red 紅	pink 粉紅
orange 橘	yellow 黃
green 綠	blue 藍
purple 紫	black 黑
white 白	gray 灰
brown 褐	beige 米白
light green 淺綠	dark green 墨綠
navy blue 深藍	turquoise 藍綠
hot pink 桃紅	neon green 螢光綠
silver 銀	gold 金

英語基礎會話600

天氣（Weather）

sunny 晴天	cloudy 陰天
rainy 雨天	foggy 起霧
lightening 打雷	thunderstorm 雷雨
typhoon 颱風	

溫度（Temperature）

thermometer 溫度計	Fahrenheit 華氏
Centigrade / Celsius 攝氏	hot 熱
warm 溫暖	cool 涼爽
cold 冷	freezing 酷寒

四季（Seasons）

summer 夏季	fall / autumn 秋季
winter 冬季	spring 春季

時鐘讀法（Reading the clock）

2:00

two o'clock   two   two o'clock sharp

2:05

two five   five after two   five minutes after two

2:15

two fifteen   a quarter after two
fifteen minutes after two

英語基礎會話600

2:20

two twenty   twenty after two

twenty minutes after two

2:30

two thirty   half past two

2:40

two forty   twenty to three

twenty minutes before three

2:45

two forty-five   a quarter to three

fifteen minutes before three

2:55

two fifty-five   five to three

five minutes before three

2:00

two a.m.

14:00

two p.m.

12:00

noon   twelve noon

24:00

midnight   twelve midnight

3:00 p.m.

three p.m.   three o'clock in the afternoon

three in the afternoon

3:00 a.m.

three a.m.　　　　three o'clock in the morning
three in the morning

拼字說明 （Spelling Clarification）

當用英文與他人溝通時出了障礙或誤解時，可以用拼字的方式來澄清。

國人在講英文字母時，常常讓外國人聽不懂。可能是學習發音時學錯了，或者受了其它的影響。有幾個字母特別容易發生問題。比方說，要用英文拼出自己中文名字時，讓外國人聽不懂，而產生更多的溝通障礙。

下列就是幾組常常會念錯的字母。

G, J, Z　　念起來應該是　gee / Jay / zee

M, N　　　念起來應該是　am / Ann

F, V　　　念起來應該是　eff / vee

W　　　　念起來應該是　double u

X　　　　念起來應該是　ex

B, P　　　念起來應該是　bee / pea

L, R　　　念起來應該是　Al / are

字母代碼單字 （Phonic Alphabet）

如果一時無法把自己的發音改正，可用下面的字母單字來拼字。只要把聽不清楚的字，用字母單字代替就可以了。如果把整句話的每一個字都拼出來的話，可能一個小時也說不了幾句話。旅行社或航空界常用這種拼音法來說明機票訂位的電腦代碼，或班機航班號碼。

問句（Question）

Can you spell that, please?

你可不可以把那個（字）拼出來？

How do you spell that?

那（個字）怎麼拼？

回答（Answer）

My name is Jake, with a "J" like in "John".

我的名字是Jake（杰克）。是J，像John 裡的J。

確定拼法（Verifying a spelling）

Is that an "F" as in Frank, or a "V" like Victor?

是Frank 的 F，還是Victor 的V ？

這裡只有列出一個簡單的單字配一個字母供參考。你也可以選擇用自己比較順口的單字配字母。

A	apple	B	boy	C	Charlie
D	dog	E	Edward	F	Frank
G	George	H	Henry	I	Iris

英語基礎會話600

J	John	K	king	L	love
M	Mark	N	Nancy	O	orange
P	Peter	Q	queen	R	Robert
S	Steve	T	Tom	U	uncle
V	Victor	W	whiskey	X	X-ray
Y	yes	Z	zero		

吳炳鍾英語教室系列

英語基礎會話600

2004年12月初版　　　　　　　　　　　　　定價：新臺幣160元
2014年10月初版第九刷
有著作權・翻印必究
Printed in Taiwan.

著　　　者	吳	炳	鍾
	李	怡	慧
發　行　人	林	載	爵

出　　版　　者	聯經出版事業股份有限公司	叢書主編	何　采　嬪
地　　　　　址	台北市基隆路一段180號4樓	校　　對	林　慧　如
台北聯經書房	台北市新生南路三段94號	封面設計	陳　泰　榮
電　話	（02）23620308		
台中分公司	台中市北區崇德路一段198號		
暨門市電話	（04）22312023		
郵政劃撥帳戶第0100559-3號			
郵撥電話	（02）23620308		
印　　刷　　者	世和印製企業有限公司		
總　經　銷	聯合發行股份有限公司		
發　行　所	新北市新店區寶橋路235巷6弄6號2F		
電　話	（02）29178022		

行政院新聞局出版事業登記證局版臺業字第0130號

本書如有缺頁，破損，倒裝請寄回台北聯經書房更換。ISBN　978-957-08-2786-6 (平裝附光碟片)
聯經網址 http://www.linkingbooks.com.tw
電子信箱 e-mail:linking@udngroup.com

國家圖書館出版品預行編目資料

英語基礎會話600 / 吳炳鍾、
李怡慧合著 . --初版 .
--臺北市：聯經，2003年
136面；14.8×21公分 . （吳炳鍾英語教室）
ISBN 978-957-08-2786-6（平裝附光碟片）
[2014年10月初版第九刷]

1.英國語言-會話

805.188 930222053